DEVIL'S MISTLETOE

A DARK MAFIA ROMANCE

ROSELYN ASH
SASHA LEONE

Copyright © 2022 by Roselyn Ash & Sasha Leone

All rights reserved.

No part of this book may be reproduced in any form or by any electronic or mechanical means, including information storage and retrieval systems, without written permission from the author, except for the use of brief quotations in a book review.

For everyone obsessed with the naughtier side of Christmas, this is for you.

1

VITTORIA

It's almost Christmas, and I have no one to kiss beneath the mistletoe.

Again.

But that's the least of my worries.

My name is Vitorria Bernardino, and ever since I was a little girl, I've been watching my mother do whatever it takes to make money for us.

At first, things were going well. But after my father passed away from a drug overdose, mom changed.

I was finally starting to recover from the loss and grief, and doing well in school too, when she decided to pick up where he left off. Before I knew it, she was worse than dad ever was; hooked on drugs, as well as something much darker.

We were struggling. Hard.

Then, by some miracle, she got a job at the infamous Bianchi Manor, and I thought that just might save our lives.

But things never go as planned.

I was sixteen years old when I moved to the imposing old mansion with my mom. I'm almost eighteen now.

Despite her drug habit, mom was hired to work as a handmaid to the wife of the well-known and mysterious master of the house. I'd heard rumors that he was a ruthless mob boss, but even that didn't prepare me for what happened next... or who the real monster of the manor was.

Arianna Bianchi, his wife, is a gorgeous woman in her late thirties with glossy blonde hair and cold unrelenting blue eyes, her figure slim to the extreme—almost painfully thin. She wears the most expensive designer clothes I have ever seen, and she tosses them away after wearing them *once*.

One piece of those designer items could cover my little family's expenses for months on end. But she never gives them, or us, a second thought.

I guess that's the story of my life.

While mom worked in the house, I finished high school. And even though I liked my classes, I never had much hope for a life after that. Mostly because mom insisted that I would work in the manor once I graduated.

Or rather, *once I turned eighteen.*

That number lingers in my near future, a painful reminder that I'm expected to grow up and take care of myself very soon.

Mom's insistence that I work at the Manor dashed any hopes I'd had of going to college. I know I was foolish to hope, yet I found myself wondering what life would be like if I ever got the opportunity to study. Maybe I'd even be able to take control of my own life. But with mom going from paycheck to paycheck and doing drugs behind the house owners' backs, I knew I couldn't count on her for support or to pay for my tuition.

With the fierce competition in my class, I was coming up short.

I would never get a scholarship, and any chance I had to get away from my toxic household escaped me—that is, until my mother suddenly died in a sequence of events that changed my life forever.

It all started just before Christmas break...

I arrive home from school late, walking downstairs into the small apartment I share with my mother, to find her already entertaining visitors.

But this time, it isn't one of the sketchy guys she sometimes drags into our apartment for a few folded bills and an hour or two in her bedroom.

Nope. It's Mrs. Bianchi herself. Arianna. The lady of the Manor.

She's sitting behind our small dining table—an odd sight—her perfectly manicured nails clicking against the wood as she impatiently waits for my mother.

I feel stiff and timid as I walk in the room with her sitting there.

"What are you waiting for, *domestica*?" she immediately barks at me. "Serve me a cup of tea."

I quietly and quickly got to work, too intimidated to push back.

Even though I don't work for Arianna—technically the odd jobs I do around the house are for her husband—I'm lucky enough to be allowed under her roof. This apartment is part of the Manor, after all, and without it, mom and I would surely be homeless.

Working fast, I serve her tea in our least chipped mugs and then disappear to the bathroom to reapply the red lipstick my mother gave me a few years ago.

It's a vintage case with a garish shade of bright red hidden inside.

Strange, that such a simple gift has influenced my life so much.

I started dressing to fit the lipstick—now I wear a lot of

monochromatic colors and gothic outfits. Not that anyone cares what I wear.

Well, except maybe for...

I smile to myself.

Looking into the mirror, I think of how mom gifted me the lipstick for my fifteenth birthday. She even put on a little photoshoot so I could show it off. I tried to look my best for her, smiling just like I am now.

One of the photographs sits framed right above the TV. In my mind, it's one of the last signs that she still actually cares about me.

My smile fades, and I swallow thickly as I close the lipstick tube, my hands shaky.

Mom doesn't show me much affection anymore. Not that she ever really did. Still, it used to be better than this—at least, I think.

I take my time in the bathroom, but once I make it back to the kitchen, I notice mom has reappeared. She's accompanied by a man who can't seem to keep his eyes off Mrs. Bianchi. I shudder at the thought of his attention, but Mrs. Bianchi hardly seems bothered. In fact, she seems to enjoy it, even despite his disheveled appearance, pot belly, and the fact that I can smell the alcohol on him from here. Her laughter fills our little apartment as she giggles along to all his corny, lewd jokes.

The second mom notices me, though, I'm hurried out of the kitchen, and I go back to the small bedroom we share, somewhat relieved.

I glance at the rumpled sheets on her bed and make my way to mine, pulling over the curtain that separates me from whatever mom does on her side of the room.

Once again, I open the small tube of lipstick and dab it on my lips. It's becoming a nervous habit.

It's a bright, daring shade of red called Pure Seduction.

Devil's Mistletoe

When I turned fifteen, it felt especially cool to get lipstick from my mom.

It stood out from the other girls' pink and brown shades. But as I got older, I started to realize how inappropriate it was... especially when I was doing small tasks around the house and I could feel Mr. Bianchi's gaze on me.

I sigh.

Mr. Bianchi.

The mysterious head of the house who runs this place with an iron fist. I think about him often.

He's always nice to me, even if we only rarely cross paths.

That's changed lately, especially in the last few weeks. Sometimes I can feel him staring at me, tapping his fingers impatiently when I'm nearby. Even though he remains perfectly polite, I can tell something has changed. I just don't know what.

Part of me is afraid he'll become just like his wife. Mrs. Bianchi is always ready to reprimand me for the smallest of things. I really hope nothing like that happens with him.

It would just make my sad little life that much sadder.

Sitting down at my rickety little desk, I busy myself by drawing a few designs in my sketchbook. It's my prized possession, even more so than the lipstick from mom. I bought it with money I made from doing small side jobs for Mr. Bianchi.

For the past few months, I've kept these jobs a secret from mom, because I'm afraid if she finds out, she's going to take the money away for herself.

I haven't bought anything inappropriate with it, just some fabric and the sketchbook. I love drawing my designs out on the models before I start working on them. And fabric is so expensive that I want to practice first. I can't afford to make mistakes.

I sew all my own clothes by hand because I can't really

afford the expensive designs they sell at stores in the city. Besides, I don't really like what's selling these days.

According to mom, my designs are old fashioned, but ever since I started noticing Mr. Bianchi's silent appreciation of how the outfits look on me, I've started to be a little less... *modest* with them, making the dresses and skirts shorter and tighter.

I started edging my hemlines with lace and added pearls to the collars of my shirts. I've even started cinching my waist in, because I always notice how Mr. Bianchi looks at me when I do that.

Now that my dresses are shorter, I'll often wear them with tights or even stockings if I'm feeling extra brave. And more than a few times, I've noticed *him* staring at me as I've bent over.

Sometimes, I even bend over just for him.

As ashamed as I am of the forbidden feeling that takes over me every single time that happens, I can't seem to stop myself. I can't help but bait him, trying desperately to get more of his attention.

I know he's married and I know my mother would lose it if she ever found out what I was doing. Worst of all, I would have no explanation to give her—even *I* don't understand why I'm so obsessed with him.

Honestly, it's probably best I don't think about it too much. So, instead, I stay focused on my sketchbook—that is, until I hear our front door slam shut.

I only make my way back to the kitchen when I'm sure everybody has left.

Sure enough, the place is empty. My mom's gone for the day, and that feels strange—she barely leaves the apartment we live in, other than for work, of course. Quite often, though, we have visitors at the house.

Which is why I've made the Manor's library my silent comfort zone.

So far, nobody's noticed that I spend a lot of time there.

Even late at night when everybody else is asleep. But I'm sure that if Mr. Bianchi or Mrs. Bianchi found out, they would *not* be pleased with me sneaking upstairs, especially when everybody knows that it's *not* allowed for the help.

Still, sometimes I can hardly bear to stay in the apartment.

I feel like it always smells like the last man my mother was with.

Smoothing down my dress, I pace our room. I can't go upstairs now because somebody might catch me. It's too early in the day. Instead, I curl up on my bed, the one private corner I have, and pull out my mother's laptop.

She would hate that I'm using it, but I have no phone and I'm desperate to find out what's going on in the world. We don't even have a TV—it died a few months ago and mom never got around to replacing it.

Sometimes I'll hear what happens downtown from the other servants in the house, or in passing from someone we work for, but most of the time I'm pretty out of touch with the outside world, especially now that I'm nearly finished with school.

The Bianchi Manor stands on a large private piece of land, and there is no one around for miles. It's rare that I have enough money to head into the city—it takes hours. Plus, I'm a little afraid of going around there on my own. I hear the crime downtown is getting worse every day.

I've seen what kind of guys my mom brings to the house, and lately, I've been getting more and more afraid that she's going to want to involve me in her *business*. Especially since I'm turning eighteen very soon.

Holding myself, I try to relax in our small apartment, but peace of mind escapes me. I'm struggling to focus on anything other than my upcoming birthday.

I finally settle in the kitchen, with a steaming cup of tea warming my palms. I tell myself mom would never involve me in the business she runs, but even as I say it to myself, I know that's not true.

Even the lipstick she gave me was inappropriate for my age. It feels like a gift designed to make me ready for a life she wants me to lead. I'm extra worried now that I've seen Arianna Bianchi in our apartment.

It's starting to make me wonder what they have planned for me.

Mom has never hidden her opinions on college—according to her, it's out of the question. Instead, after I turn eighteen, she expects me to start working in the Manor full-time, just like she does.

One day, I'd like to move out on my own. I've always dreamt of an apartment that I don't have to share with my mother; of having my own bedroom. I'm desperate to know what it's like to have some privacy.

Especially now, when my most recent thoughts have been invaded by Mr. Bianchi.

My mind is filled with fantasies of running off somewhere alone with him. I've tried not to entertain that idea for too long, though. It's simply too tempting, and Mr. Bianchi is a married man—no matter how smoking hot he is when he looks at me with his brows furrowed.

Still, in the past few months, I've started hopelessly searching for roommate postings in apartments downtown. I managed to find a few addresses, which I scribbled down on a piece of paper and hid in the kitchen drawer. Sometimes, when I'm anxious, I like to look at them and daydream about being able to afford such a thing.

That'll be the day.

Placing my tea aside, I go to search for that piece of paper. I made sure to stuff it in the very back of the drawer, where we keep all of the instruction manuals, because I know mom never looks in there.

But when I reach all the way in the back and pull it out, I realize it's been scrunched up.

I never did that.

My heart drops.

Did someone see it?

My pulse starts to race as I rifle through the drawer, looking for clues. But all I find are pictures of me, leftovers from the photoshoot we had on my birthday. These ones aren't like the one that's been framed above the TV in the living room, though.

With my heart still pounding, I take a good look at one of the photos and notice that my bra strap is hanging all the way down my shoulder. And my tank top is exposing more of my pale skin than I'm comfortable with.

I flip the picture over and find a note written in my mom's curly cursive.

Ten thousand dollars.

More money than I've seen in my entire life, and more than I could ever hope to earn in a year.

But what does it mean?

I look at the rest of the details listed below the number. There's my age, weight, my eye color, my hair color…

And the fact that I'm a virgin.

I let go of the picture as if I've been burned by its sharp edges. Robotically, I put it back into the kitchen drawer and slam it shut.

I can't believe what I've just seen—even though I can pretty much tell what it's all about.

No. Mom wouldn't. She couldn't.

Could she?

When I wake up, it's hours later and it's raining outside.

Mom still isn't home, but right now, I'm grateful for it.

The last thing I want to do is talk to her about my discovery in the kitchen drawer.

I don't feel safe. I know when she comes home, she'll realize I found out her plan for me.

It was never easy for me to keep a secret. Everyone says they can read my face like an open book. Mom will be able to tell right away. She knows me better than anyone.

I can't stay here. But it's not like I have anywhere to go... except maybe the library. It should be empty for the night, and I always feel more comfortable there.

Gathering up a little courage, I dash from the apartment and run upstairs.

A well-practiced habit by now.

Before I can reach my destination, though, I notice one of the lights is on in the hallway up there.

That's unusual, so I hide behind the brocade curtains in the lobby and watch with bated breath.

That's when I see mom.

It's not unusual for her to be helping Mrs. Bianchi this late, but they'd usually be downstairs, hiding from Mr. Bianchi.

I can tell something's wrong—my mother seems distressed as she walks up against the banister separating her from the ground floor, her back hitting the marble railing.

My racing pulse stops dead when I see a shadowy figure appear in front of her. She lets out a shriek, and I can't help but step out from the shadows, heart pumping with fear.

Before I can react, the shadowy figure pushes her over the banister.

All I can do is watch with horror as her body tumbles to the hardwood floor.

She hits with a loud crack. Then everything goes silent.

I hear her weakly cry out.

I try to make my legs move, to run up to her, check if she's okay, but before I can, the person who pushed her steps down the stairs.

I immediately recognize him.

Alessio Giordano, Mr. Bianchi's best friend.

I want to do something. Anything. Scream. Help. Fight. But I'm a coward. I just stand there as Alessio walks up to mom's twitching body and shoots her in the forehead.

The gunshot echoes through the lobby like thunder.

I don't know how long I'm standing there before I snap out of it, but when I do, all I can do is turn and run, my steps echoing in the empty hallway behind me; my dream of the library all to myself long forgotten.

2

DOMENICO

It didn't take me long to realize Arianna won't be the wife I've always wanted.

Our marriage was always one of convenience, arranged and set up by myself and her father.

She's my age, beautiful, blonde, and painfully thin—so thin that at one point, I was worried she might keel over and die on me.

I don't really worry about that anymore—in fact, I often hope she does.

It's hard to say we grew apart, because we were never close to begin with. Arianna's hated me ever since our wedding night, when she took off her wedding gown to show me the gorgeous bridal lingerie she was wearing underneath it.

But I wasn't interested.

I broke her heart and told her our marriage was never going to be consummated. I didn't want children—at least, not with her.

She took that hard. And for a while, I almost felt bad for her. But that sympathy's long gone now. And Arianna pretends she doesn't care anymore.

No matter how many times she tried to seduce me into something resembling a romantic relationship, I denied her. And the more I did, the uglier she became.

Or maybe she was always ugly inside, and my rejection just brought it out from hiding.

It doesn't matter. I wasn't interested in all that, not with her. Hell, not with anyone.

But that all changed when *Vittoria* moved into the Manor.

Ever since that little maid moved in, I've been unhealthily obsessed with her.

Fucking hell.

Vittoria dresses in the most delightful gothic outfits I've ever seen. She manages to inject a modern twist into the classics, which is unlike anything I've seen on runways. And I've seen my share of models.

I know she sews her own clothes too, and I'm baffled by it all.

Her talents are bigger than the life she's trapped in.

Sometimes, I secretly go through her sketchbook and look at the designs and models she's put in there. She's got an amazing eye, not just for textures, but for finding patterns that work seamlessly together. I love how everything she puts together is so very girly.

That feminine side of her gets me off more than anything else. Almost as much as her barely legal, ripe-for-the-taking age.

I put on my suit jacket and inspect myself in the full-length mirror in my study.

I wonder how Vittoria sees me.

Does she see what everyone else does, or can she look past my tall, dark and dangerous physique?

Has she paid enough attention to notice I'm tattooed with kinky BDSM scenes, featuring skeletons in various sex positions with faceless women?

I never had the faces done on those tattoos because I never met a woman I wanted to be on me for the rest of my life.

Still, I held out hope that I'd meet that woman one day. Then I'd have all the faces filled in with hers.

It's ironic that I married, and never had my wife's face added onto them. But Arianna is nothing more to me than a contract. I never feel any passion when it comes to her, even though I know she is desperate to get into my bed.

Yeah, like that would ever happen.

I see her more as an obstacle than my wife these days.

She served her purpose, furthering my business relationship with some of the other mafia families in the city, but now I'm fucking done with that, and she's boring me—especially since I realize I can't have Vittoria unless I end things with her.

It's not like Arianna's made the choice hard for me. She's been bragging about her cheating escapades for years now. And she's been growing increasingly bitter ever since Vittoria came to live at the Manor.

I must not be hiding my obsession as well as I hoped.

Oh well.

I take another long look at myself in the mirror. The grey specks in my blue eyes almost match my hair now. The salt and pepper look is quickly giving way to pure salt.

I fucking hate that.

I look so much older.

Sneering, I trace the back of my fingers down my chiseled jaw. It's covered in a thin layer of stubble, and I wonder if Vittoria has ever felt a man's facial hair before.

Well, if she wanted to feel mine, she'd need a ladder.

I stand at 6'8", towering over not just my wife, but my pretty little maid, too.

Perhaps the *true* reason I never take Arianna seriously is because she never gives me the feeling that I need to take care of her.

It's different with Vittoria, though. She clearly craves my attention. It's not like her little games have gone unnoticed. For a girl who toys with my cock so much, she sure as fuck hasn't spent enough time touching it.

But she will. Soon.

I've spent countless moments dreaming about hearing the word I most want to hear ripping itself from her lips when she least expects it to.

I wonder whether she'll be one of those girls who say it of their own accord.

I want her to whisper *daddy* in my ear when she's at her most irresistible. When I can wrap my hand around her long neck and prevent her from speaking again as I pound my baby into her belly.

I button my suit jacket and step away from the mirror. Any kind of fate I have in mind for Vittoria is much better than what her mother would've done with her.

I found out about the woman's nasty plans a few weeks ago, and ever since then, I've known what I have to do.

That's why I arranged to have Vittoria's mother, Sophia, murdered.

And I knew exactly who to trust with the mission—my best friend Alessio Giordano.

Ah, Alessio.

I'd taken the bright-eyed killer in a few years ago. He was a little younger than me, and I knew his father, but we got along well enough.

Still, I never thought much of Alessio until his family was massacred in a horrific murder.

It was enough to kill any man. And everyone assumed Alessio was among the victims, including me.

When he showed up on my doorstep, he'd lost all his memories and developed a form of amnesia where he would forget things every time he fell asleep.

I gave him a place to stay and recover in. I sheltered him from his enemies. Now he's returning the favor.

Sure, we grew apart over the last few months—especially since Vittoria came to live with me—but I still trusted Alessio completely. He's like a brother to me.

Suddenly, my phone rings with an incoming call. I see Alessio's number flashing across the screen, and I pick it up with a cheerful smile.

"How's work?" I ask, smirking to myself as I think of Vittoria.

Freshly orphaned and at my disposal, with everything taken care of. Fucking delightful.

Hopefully no complications.

Alessio grunts on the other side. "Job's done. Anything else you'd like me to do for you?"

I responded with an easy chuckle. "Good work. I'll call you when I need something else."

"Figures. You only call me when you need something, is that it?"

"When it comes to her... yes. I'll call you when she's 18."

"Don't tell me your mind is still on that pretty little maid?" Alessio asks, laughing.

"Why else would I do this?" I say, raising an eyebrow.

"You sure go to some extreme lengths to get the girl you want," Alessio says, and I can feel him shaking his head on the other end of the line.

"I bet you'll be the same once you find someone."

"Doubtful," he hisses. "Although your maid sure is pretty."

Almost without thinking, my fingers curl up into a possessive fist.

"Watch yourself, Alessio. She's mine. I already told you that."

"Yeah yeah yeah," he sighs. "Our little game of dibs is still fully on, I haven't forgotten. She's yours."

"Good to know you haven't completely lost your mind... yet. Speak soon, Alessio," I mutter. "Thank you."

I cut the call.

But I can't shake what Alessio said. He's right. My obsession has reached new extremes.

It's not like there's anyone else that could hold my attention apart from Vittoria. I am well and truly obsessed, every waking thought consumed by the redhead maid who always wears her hair in braids.

After I found out from my wife that Vittoria's mother was planning on selling her virginity in an online auction, and that she'd even taken photos of her in preparation, I knew I had to get rid of the bad influence in her life. I am also well aware that my red mist is descending again, and I'm being crazy protective over this girl, whom I barely even know.

I'm also married to another woman. I can't help myself, though—arranging for the murder of Vittoria's mother was a piece of cake. Alessio didn't ask any questions. He never does.

Now, I have to deliver the news to Vittoria—that she is now an orphan. And until her eighteenth birthday, she will be in my care as my ward.

I can't wait to tell her.

Moments later, I knock on the door of her apartment and am surprised when it opens instantly. I come face-to-face with my beautiful girl, her hair for once not tied up in braids but instead falling down her back in silky waves.

She's wearing that silly red lipstick. I don't know how to feel about it, because while I do like the shade, I can't help but associate it with her mother, who also wore a similar one.

An urge overtakes me—to wipe the offending color off her mouth, and then make her suck my thumb. But I force myself not to think about it.

Instead, I walk inside.

I'm immediately shocked by the state of the apartment. I

don't visit often, but it's taken a turn for the worse since I was last here. It certainly didn't look this way when we gave it to Vittoria's mother.

"Can I offer you a cup of tea, Sir?" my girl asks nervously, running around the kitchen as I take a seat at the small, dingy dining table. I wonder where the real wooden table has gone. I realize with an annoyed shock that Vittoria's mom must have sold it for money.

I knew about Sophia's little drug habit. I even know Arianna indulged in it. But I allowed it to happen because it kept Arianna off my back. Plus, I never thought it was my problem—not until it put Vittoria at risk. Then it started to piss me off.

I scratch at a dent in the table.

Vittoria presents me with a cup, her hand shaking so much, she spills hot liquid over the rim.

I lay a hand on hers, and miraculously her fingers stop shaking.

"Don't worry," I say softly. "Nothing bad is going to happen to you. I promise, Vittoria."

She nods, not meeting my gaze as she sits down in front of me.

"I came to tell you that your mother was found dead this morning. Apparently, she fell off the top of the stairs."

I feel bad for delivering such awful news in such a matter-of-fact voice, but I don't know how else to tell her that she is free.

If Vittoria knows as much about her mother as I do, she'll surely be relieved to be free of her clutches.

I watch her reaction closely.

Besides, I don't want to spoil the rest of her life. I only want her to be free of the people who want to harm her.

"I know this must be hard to hear," I say softly, even though Vittoria hasn't reacted to my words at all.

I'm surprised by her nonchalance. I wonder whether she

made peace with her mother's death a long time ago. She certainly doesn't show any surprise that the vile woman is gone.

"You will turn 18 in a few weeks. Is that correct?" I ask Vittoria, and she nods, still refusing to meet my gaze.

I'm damn tempted to reach forward, grab her by the chin and force her to look at me, but I know it's too soon for that.

"Until then, I can take you in as my ward," I suggest. "Once you turn 18, things will change for you, but let's give it some time until then, to adjust. You can start working in the house full-time to earn your keep. You will receive the same wage as your mother did. Nothing has to change. We just have to wait for your birthday."

"You would be prepared to do that for me, Sir?" she asks softly.

"Of course," I nod gravely. "You have no one left in the world, and I have a responsibility to you."

I refuse to explain the full state of my emotions to Vittoria. She's not ready for that yet.

"Thank you, Sir," she says.

It's the first time since I told her that her mother died that I see a trace of tears welling in her beautiful eyes.

I wish more than ever that I could wipe them away, but instead, I force myself to pull the chair away from the table, rather forcefully.

I stand up and leave her alone in the apartment, wishing I could stay. But I don't fucking trust myself around Vittoria.

Once I'm outside, I bang my fist against the wall in the hallway with frustration.

If only Arianna didn't exist, then I could make Vittoria mine *now*. But I have to resist.

Just a little while longer.

3

DOMENICO

3 weeks later...

Some would say she's been sent here to test my patience.

Little do they know I have none left when it comes to Vittoria Bernardino.

She may be a temptress, but she's *my* temptress.

My wife is nagging me again, but I've already tuned out her voice, focusing instead on my finally-old-enough maid pouring Arianna one of her numerous daily cocktails. Christmas-themed today.

It's Vittoria's birthday. Not that she got to celebrate. Arianna worked her raw today.

Vittoria leans over to fix an ornament on the Christmas tree, giving me a full view of her peachy ass in the uniform I ordered specifically for her. She brings herself back up and I turn my eyes away from the forbidden little piece of ass, focusing instead on her lightly flushed, pale face.

Vittoria catches me looking. A hidden giggle escapes her lips. It's like music to my ears. The ornament sparkles.

I adjust my pants.

I can't wait for Arianna to fuck off with her next affair partner. Ever since I told her she's a business alliance, and that our marriage is a farce, she's been out fucking half the town.

But I won't let her take it out on Vittoria.

It's fucking late, and the girl should be in bed.

Damn Arianna's attitude.

Still, not even my nagging wife can deflect my attention. I'm still focused on Vittoria.

I can tell her outfit is uncomfortable for her. I know that because I made sure it was.

Now, there's one last thing standing in my way before I can make Vittoria mine. One last task and I will own her completely.

I tune out my wife's incessant voice as I think about ordering the dress for Vittoria. I had her measured by a professional seamstress, only so I could get her a dress that was a little too small.

As I watch her struggle to pull the hem down, I once again congratulate myself on such a brilliant idea.

Mr Domenico, I'm scared my dress is a little... inappropriate?

Her voice rings out in my head and I smirk to myself, remembering how carefully I reassured her that she looked perfect in her deliberately tiny outfit.

My hand tightens into a fist. I've waited for two years. It's all finally about to pay off.

Tick tock, I think as I look at my wife. *Time's almost up.*

"Are you even listening to me?" Arianna asks, crossing her arms defensively, no doubt in an attempt to get me to stare at her obscenely displayed tits. "Hello? Earth to Domenico? Wouldn't hurt to give your wife some attention like you're giving the damn *domestica*, you know. Or have you forgotten that she's a fucking maid!"

Vittoria flushes and quickly looks away from me, as if she's been caught doing something forbidden.

Damn you, Arianna.

"Try being more interesting then," I hiss. "Your boring stories are making me want to shoot myself. Are we done here?"

"Oh, we are absolutely done," Arianna says with a nasty tone. "Since you aren't even listening, I'll get going. Why don't you call your orphan pal over? I'm going out, anyway!"

She grabs her fur coat off the leather couch and Vittoria struggles to catch up with her, trying to help her put it on.

"Don't you dare insult Alessio," I sneer.

"You mean your little hound dog?" she smirks, pushing Vittoria away.

I pick myself up, seeing red. I'm tired of seeing my wife use my next and final bride like a puppet on strings.

That's my fucking job.

Luckily, I won't have to put up with it much longer. I've made up my mind.

Discreetly, I type a message into my phone—a signal that will set my plan into motion.

I smile forcefully at my wife.

"Maybe you'll change your mind about him," I say. "See you around, Arianna. Have fun tonight."

"You're not even a little bit jealous?" she asks, puckering her lips unattractively. "Not going to ask who I'm going out with?"

"Of course I am," I reply, practically roaring the words just so she'll get out of my way and I can get a better look at Vittoria. "You need to get going, though. Don't want to be late, do you?"

Arianna challenges me with a cold stare, but I don't relent. I open the door for her and gently lead her out of the room before she can cause any more chaos.

I can feel Vittoria blushing from all the way by the door.

The heat coming off her body is undeniable as she tries to look at anything but me. I struggle to keep my eyes off her as well.

But first I have to make sure my wife is out of the house.

I watch Arianna walk down to the chauffeur who's already waiting for her with one of our Bentleys. She gives me one last stare through the window and then smiles, waving like she's in some damn pageant.

She truly has no idea what kind of men she's about to see tonight. It won't be like her usual johns. But I don't give a damn anymore.

I slam the front door shut and saunter back upstairs into my office.

Vittoria patiently waits for me, Arianna's unfinished drink in her hand. I watch her silently take me in, swallowing thickly as she realizes I've come to stay this time.

She's been so nervous around me lately, but all it does is fill me with more desire to make her mine, once and for all.

I've been so fucking patient for the last two years. More patient than a goddamn saint, waiting even though it tested every primal instinct in me. Well, there's no more ignoring my need to protect this girl at all costs or my overwhelming desire to just take over her life.

It's time.

Yes, having Vittoria around the house was an exercise in patience. But with her birthday today, I am fucking done resisting.

My life will never be the same. Neither will Vittoria's.

And as for my wife?

Well, her life is about to end.

The kill order I put out on her will make sure of that. I breathe a sigh of relief, knowing that I won't ever have to listen to her nagging ever again.

I smile to myself.

Ruthless?

Damn fucking right I am.

If I was a better man, I would regret sending Alessio after Arianna. But I am already excited about her comeuppance.

She has taunted me with her affairs ever since Vittoria came to the Manor. It wasn't hard to figure out she was cheating. It's not like Arianna is exactly covert about her operations. But even if she was, I know everything that happens in the city. I have enough eyes around to ensure the walls have ears. I rule the damn place, after all.

And now, I will rule my pretty little maid too.

As I look at Vittoria shivering before me, I realize I can't keep up this game anymore.

She's definitely afraid of me, and I want some semblance of consent before I make her mine. It's the right thing to do.

She yawns discreetly.

"Is my wife overworking you again, Vittoria?" I say, shaking my head as I look at her. "It's damn near two a.m. so we need to get you to sleep. But tell me... how does it feel?"

"How does what feel, Sir?," she asks quietly as if she's still afraid to speak in my presence.

"Being eighteen," I smile.

"Oh..." she flushes and it's adorable. "Not much different. I'm just tired. And your wife hasn't been too mean, Sir."

"Don't lie to me, *ragazza*," I demand, approaching her before realizing I'm overstepping already. "She's gone now. You can be honest."

She hesitates.

The moment our eyes meet seems to last forever.

I need to be gentle around her, but it's damn near unnaturally hard for me. I've never dealt with such a delicate creature.

"Maybe she is a bit demanding," she whispers breathlessly.

Despite my inner desire to reach forward and tuck a strand of hair behind her ear, I force myself to keep looking at her and commit every feature on her gorgeous face to memory.

The way her lip curves. The doll-like Cupid's bow that's been sending my head into a tailspin for the past two years. Her too short black and white uniform that reveals the perfect globes of her ass every time she bends over.

I'm tempted to tell her to do that now, but I just barely manage to hold myself back.

"Go on," I encourage her gently.

Consent, I remind myself. *Important, at least for the first time.*

I don't want her to run off on me before everything's even started. I need to put the game in place. Vittoria can't know I've had her *mother* killed, much less my *wife*.

"It's nothing," she shakes her head. "Sorry, Sir. Do you mind if I get some rest? It's my first birthday without my mother and... I suppose I feel lonely. It's almost Christmas..."

I smile.

It's been about three weeks since Vittoria's mother was put six feet under, right where she belongs.

I stood next to Vittoria by the grave and watched her throw a rose on her mother's casket. My *ragazza* shed a single tear. That was one more tear than the woman deserved. At least it was just one. The rest would be saved for me, and *only* me.

I look at her again and pull myself to go back to the present. But every time I look at Vittoria, my thoughts go to places I've done my best to avoid for the past two years.

Now that I know she's ripe for my taking, I can't hold off for much longer.

With Arianna out of the house, I won't last.

"I think you should get some rest," I say abruptly. "Today was a big day. Birthdays are always exhausting. Perhaps you'll get a belated chance to celebrate tomorrow. Why don't you go into one of the guest bedrooms tonight? I have just the one in mind for you."

"The guest bedrooms, Sir?" Vittoria asks, her eyebrows rising in a cute way that makes me want to pet her like an adorable puppy. "I don't think that's exactly appropriate. None of this stuff is allowed—to sleep upstairs, you know?"

She giggles nervously.

"They warned us about it on my first day," she finishes shyly. "A girl got busted sleeping in one of the beds and she got fired."

I remember the annoying incident.

But that maid didn't get canned for sleeping in any bed. She got sent away because she tried to sleep in the Master's bed.

In my bed.

And no one was allowed to do that but me... until now.

I didn't covet her like I do Vittoria.

"Nonsense," I say, smirking at her. "The only person you need to listen to is me, *ragazza*."

A strong urge to kiss the top of her nose takes over me, but I don't let it lead me into an impulsive decision. Instead, I motion for her to follow me. She does, ever obedient, and I show her to the guest bedroom I think she will like best.

It's a dark room with rose-patterned wallpaper and deep navy and black tones. The print reminds me of the dresses Vittoria wears when she isn't squirming in an obscenely tiny uniform.

I've caught glimpses of them on her days off. They're cute little numbers, designed and hand-sewn by her. I offered to buy her a sewing machine once, but she said she prefers doing it by hand.

Often, she'll use velvet, but she also likes lace—black, white or anything jewel-toned, always combining monochromatic colors with fun girly accents that drive me wild.

As if that's not enough, her hair is always braided into two pigtails too, giving me ideas I'm only now allowed to entertain.

I don't know whether or not I've been imagining it, but I have a feeling lately, she's been making the designs shorter and shorter to catch my attention on purpose.

Maybe it's because she's seen my reaction to the naughty little uniform I picked out for her. I think she secretly likes it.

"Sir, I really don't think this is okay," she says. "Do I really look that tired?"

"You look like you could use a good night's rest," I tell her with an insistent smile, even though it's a straight-up lie.

She looks damn near perfect to me. I'm just using her yawn as an excuse to get her in bed. While she sleeps, there are a few other inconveniences I need to take care of.

Still, I can't resist the thought of her just a couple of doors away from my bedroom. Already, my head is filling with fantasies.

I could send the rest of the staff on a forced vacation day...

Yes, that's exactly what I'll do. Then I'll have Vittoria all to myself.

Ragazza chuckles nervously, as if she doesn't fully understand why I'm having her go to bed, especially here. But then she yawns again.

I shut the curtains and motion to the bed. It's covered in a luxurious faux fur throw.

"You deserve it," I say. "Only the best. Get some rest and get back to work in the morning. I'll deal with everything else."

I walk out of the room without giving her a second glance, and as quietly as I can, I lock the door behind me, ensuring that she's safe. And that she can't run away.

There will be no escaping me this time.

Filled with satisfaction, I walk down the hallway and send another message to the head of the household, Alexander, who runs all the daily operations in the house.

I know if I send in my code, he will be able to dismiss everyone that works for me in a matter of minutes.

The staff will be pissed, because it's so close to the annual Christmas party, but they won't have much of a choice, either.

My word is the law.

As if on cue, I hear doors opening and shutting as various people leave the house. Soon enough I feel the presence of nobody but Vittoria, locked safely in her bedroom and yet still smelling so sweet, so forbidden.

One more night and then she's all mine.

Sleep escapes me later that night, and even though I know I should wait, I can't bring myself to stay away from Vittoria for much longer.

I toss and turn until five a.m. before finally giving up.

My feet carry me over the hallway, and I stop before putting the key into the lock and gently turning it to the side. I let myself in, hoping she doesn't notice my arrival. I quickly notice her shape underneath the sheets.

Vittoria is breathing slowly and I can tell she's deeply asleep. It's exactly what I want.

I approach the bed and gently pull on the covers preventing me from marveling at her body. As soon as her perfect skin comes into view, I start to lose it.

I didn't expect her to sleep fucking *naked*. But I'm glad she did.

I take in her body from above. That pale, porcelain shade continues on her rosy nipples and pussy lips.

I should have known her nipples would be pink. She has red hair and a fair coloring, but I never thought about her that way. I had to resist all those thoughts. Lock them up and throw away the key. She was much too young then.

But now?

She's eighteen—ripe to become mine.

I can't believe I abstained for so long.

My wife is gone now, confirmed by a text message from Alessio. I'm done waiting.

Once I gently pry away the covers from her body, I start exploring it with my eyes. I don't know what I expected, but it certainly wasn't this—a display of perfection, laid softly in the bed waiting just for me. It's more beautiful than any art I've ever seen.

I want to encapsulate this moment just for myself. Nobody else should get to witness such beauty. She's mine.

I can barely resist, yet I want to save this moment for when she's awake. When she can feel my fingertips searching her searing hot skin and imagine what it'll be like once I finally force them inside her.

I allow myself one long, lingering look at her naked body and something tells me I was right.

Nobody's had her before. Nobody's touched her. Somehow, one look at her perfect unspoiled body has completely convinced me that she's never been with a man in her life.

Smiling affectionately to myself, I run a finger down the split of her lips and watch as her mouth opens in a soft moan. I quickly retract my hand, afraid she's going to wake up, but the next moment, her breaths go labored and soft again.

It emboldens me to reach forward for one more touch.

This time my fingertip is focused on grazing her soft wet opening.

I desperately want to push inside and check if she's a virgin. But I have more self-control than I expected. I want to leave that surprise for both of us.

But there's something else I can do.

I pull down my boxers and bring out my cock. It feels thick and heavy in my palm, fisting it as precum runs down my shaft.

Getting off to her in person is better than anything I've felt before. My cock glistens with wetness as I coax out drops of my arousal for her.

I can't stop now. My cock is too hard, already twitching with the need to release my pent-up orgasm all over her innocent body.

I don't force myself to stop like I always do when I think of her.

No, instead I force myself to finish all over her creamy, unspoiled skin.

I watch with satisfaction as my load sprays over her body. I grunt out my release and watch as she squirms in her sleep.

I'm so goddamn tempted to reach down and touch what's mine.

No. I've already taken enough.

With one last lingering look at her sleeping form in the bed, I go back to my bedroom only a couple of doors down. It's tempting to sleep next to her, but I can't let myself do that *again*. Not without her knowing.

I do make sure to lock her bedroom, though.

Because I'm never letting her go.

4

VITTORIA

I wake up in the softest, most comfortable bed I've ever slept in as Christmas melodies gently play in the hallway.

This place is a sharp contrast to the maid's quarters, that's for sure.

Not that the beds aren't this comfortable down there, but this one is on another level. Pure luxury. I imagine this is what Domenico's life must be like on a daily basis. Comfort, style and money. Everything's easy for the rich and beautiful.

The moment I think of Domenico, I curse inwardly and let out a deep sigh. I was *so* hopeful yesterday, showing off for him in front of his wife shamelessly, hoping she wouldn't say a word about my clear provocations.

She barely did, only getting a little dig out before she was sent away, even though I flirted with him openly sometimes.

When Arianna rushed out, I was secretly relieved. Then, I was shocked by Domenico's proposition to let me spend the night in one of the guest rooms—as far as I know, none of the other maids or employees here have ever been allowed a privilege like that.

Not even my mother.

At the thought of her, I quickly cross myself. It's become my tradition, and a small excuse to myself. Because I don't really feel sorry she's dead.

I got over the death of my mother long before she actually died. She wasn't a good parent.

I had to watch her addiction spiral too many times to count, and I lost track of how many relapses she had. Every time she refused my help, it broke me a little more, until there was nothing left for me to give; none of my heart left to break, because it was all in pieces already.

Unless I was around Domenico. Sweet, cruel, older Domenico, who filled me with a strange sense of purpose that I didn't understand.

I used to just follow him around when I was younger, because he would occasionally give me some positive attention and even address me directly, unlike his wife.

He called me *ragazza*. A term that could be used for a maid, but also a young woman.

I hope he sees me as the latter.

Ever since my mom died and... well, especially since my birthday, nothing's been the same.

I can feel Domenico's lingering eyes on me and every single time I hope he'll turn his wordless stares into actions. I'm desperate to know what it feels like to have him run his fingers through my hair; to let him undo my braids and let my hair fall free so he can play with it.

I want him to wrap his fingers in my mane and keep a tight grip on my head as he pleasures himself with my mouth, holding me firmly in place so I don't have much of a choice.

I've never done that before, but I have a feeling I would be a good girl for him. I've been practicing. For him.

Once, I found Domenico's open computer. There was still a tab open. I looked.

I shouldn't have.

What I came across was the most brutal thing I've ever seen. The man in the video took the woman almost by *force,* but she seemed to be enjoying every second of it. More and more powerful orgasms ripped themselves from her body as she surrendered to this *beast.*

He continued this heated attack and, before I could stop myself, I slipped my fingers into my panties and started getting off on the idea of this man. Except, in my mind, the man was replaced by Domenico. And I was his good little girl. His *ragazza,* like he always said.

That was the first time I thought of him by his first name—and I try not to do that even though it comes so damn naturally to me now. I have started thinking of him so much it feels like we are the closest of friends

I know exactly how he likes his coffee in the morning and what his favorite drink is in the evening. I know he likes to kick his feet up and relax with a good book when the sun is setting outside. He loves the view of the sunset, so I often find myself watching it as well, picturing him doing the same, maybe thinking of me.

I am forever thinking of him.

I push my feet out of the bed, burying them in the soft carpet.

This must be heaven.

When I walk outside, I find the hallway deserted. It isn't uncommon for Mr. Bianchi to send all of his employees away, but it is strange because *I'm* still here. Why haven't I been sent away with the others?

As I'm making my way downstairs into the staff's corners, I run into one of the other maids, Cecilia. We never really got along because the boy she likes, who works in the stables, once had a crush on me. Ever since then, she's always found a way to be annoyed by my presence.

The truth is, I never gave that boy the time of day, but that didn't stop Cecilia from hating me. Sometimes, I can see her shooting daggers at my back when she thinks I'm not looking.

But now, she looks crestfallen, her face deathly pale as she turns her wide eyes to meet mine.

"Vittoria! Have you heard?" she asks, voice shaky.

"Heard what?"

I approach, laying a hand on her shoulder as I try to steady her.

"Goodness, Cecilia, you're shaking all over. What happened?"

"Mrs. Bianchi is dead," she whispers.

I take a step back.

"What do you mean she's dead?"

"It was a murder-suicide with her secret lover," she whispers. "Mr. Bianchi had everyone sent out of here last night, and he doesn't want us to return. A lot of us have had to sneak in to get some of our things because otherwise we'd be gone with nothing!"

She shakes her head.

"Who knows when he'll let us back. He must be consumed by grief."

He doesn't seem that sad to me.

Cecilia gives me a weird look.

"What are you doing here anyway?" she demands. "I thought we all got kicked out of here last night?"

"Not me," I shrug. "Domen-I mean, Mr. Bianchi, told me to sleep in one of the guest bedrooms last night."

"What?!"

She acts outraged, as if I just told her a cruel joke.

"But that's against protocol!"

"Well, I figured since he told me directly, it was fine," I say nervously, my hands fidgeting as I wonder if I'm going to get in trouble for this.

"Maybe he wants to get it on with you," Cecilia says, winking at me. "Although I can't see why he'd pick *you*."

I ignore the inner urge to roll my eyes as I give her a sweet smile.

"You said he kicked you out of the house, didn't you? He wouldn't be too happy that you're still here and talking to me that way. Wouldn't want me to tell him, would you, Cecilia? Since he likes me so much..."

Her eyes narrow into tiny slits.

I can tell she's pissed off, but I'm not about to give in.

Secretly, I know I've already assumed my role as the one with special attention in this house. Even though the other girls look down on me, they can tell I'm Domenico's favorite.

They wouldn't dare pick on me too much. *Would they?*

Suddenly, I feel a tall, intimidating figure appear behind me. My heartbeat quickens.

Domenico lays a heavy hand on my shoulder, and I feel dizzy all of a sudden.

"A maid?" he says. "What the hell are you doing here? I told everyone to leave and not disturb us!"

I feel a shiver crawl down my spine as his fingers dig into my skin gently.

He asserts his dominance and makes sure everybody here knows who I belong to.

... Or maybe those are just my silly fantasies, because I still haven't seen any proof of this *supposed* crush Domenico has on me.

He stares intimidatingly at Cecilia until she finally makes her exit, turning on her heels and running down the hallway after quietly mumbling an apology. She's one of those maids who's afraid to even look at him.

I can't help but giggle at that thought.

I'm not scared of Domenico Bianchi. Not anymore.

He excites me.

I don't bother to go after Cecilia to make sure she's okay.

Instead, I turn around and face the man who saved me from yet another altercation.

"It was very nice of you to let me sleep in the guest bedroom last night," I whisper, not meeting his dangerous eyes. "But I think it's going to cause some trouble with the other employees. Cecilia already reminded me that it's against protocol, and I wouldn't want it getting back to Alexander, Sir."

"You don't need to worry about him," he says, smirking at me just like in my fantasies.

Then, to my surprise, he reaches forward and brushes a strand of hair behind my ear. I'm shocked by his gentleness, and I find myself leaning into his touch, body already arching, eager for another show of his affection.

"I don't mean to pry, Sir," I say quietly as he looks at me, trying to discern what my question is going to be. "But are you... okay, Sir? I just heard what happened and it's absolutely awful."

He looks at me with a puzzled expression.

"What are you talking about, my *ragazza*?"

"Well... your wife, Sir?" I say uncertainly, my voice shaking as if half expecting him to strike me for bringing her up.

"Oh."

He groans, shaking his head with grief.

I can't help but wonder if it's genuine—not a single tear...

Surely any mortal man would cry for the wife they just lost, especially when she was caught having a secret tryst?

But not Domenico. He just stares at me intensely. That's when I realize his hand is still next to me. I lean into his palm and my hand reaches up on its own accord, wrapping around his fingers.

My lips press a gentle kiss against his palm.

I'm waiting to silently comfort him more, but he suddenly pulls back, nearly knocking over a fruit basket as he takes a few steps away from me in the hallway.

"I'm sorry, Sir," I whisper uselessly. "I overstepped."

"Don't worry about that, *ragazza*," he says, and I feel a deep desire take over my body. "Is that girl gone?"

"I could go check."

"No need. I'll ensure we're alone, then we'll talk. Tonight. One final thing I need to take care of, unfortunately."

"Tonight," I repeat, swallowing thickly. "Understood, Sir."

I can barely talk myself out of jumping on him. I've never been so needy for someone.

It's not helping that he looks better than ever today—which is strange, given that he just lost his wife.

Or maybe he's just relieved.

Arianna was finally exposed as a cheater. I bet every staff member in the house breathed their own sigh of relief when it all came out.

She was up to no good. All the servants overheard things, and they gossiped among themselves, often spreading rumors to the rest of the staff. I overheard on multiple occasions that Domenico's wife was cheating on him, but I never thought to bring it up to my boss.

I thought he knew how to deal with these things better than me. As far as I'm concerned, he knows *everything*.

He certainly has a knowing look every time he glances at me. It's almost as if he can read my innermost thoughts.

I'm afraid of his searching gaze, even now...

"I'm sorry again," I whisper. "I wanted to make you feel better."

"Oh, you did," he smirks.

"Good," I reply with more confidence than I feel. "What would you like me to do today?"

"Take the day off, but stay in the house," he rasps. "Start getting your things together."

"My things?"

"You're moving bedrooms."

"Oh, okay," I manage, nodding. "See you later then, Sir?"

Even though he's my boss—well, maybe *because* he is my boss—I'm eager to impress him and make him feel better after the tragic passing of his wife. It's the least I can do.

"See you later," he says with a smile. "Don't worry about me or Arianna. She's in a better place now. Presumably."

I can't imagine the pain... but why isn't he showing any on his handsome face?

After a few hours have passed and he hasn't sought me out, I prepare Domenica his favorite drink. I feel like a lamb to the slaughter as I rush to get everything together.

All my things are gathered in boxes. I'm hoping *so badly* that he'll let me sleep in the guest bedroom. It's beautiful, but I don't want to think about it too much. I'm scared my hopes will be dashed.

He wouldn't fire me right before Christmas, right?

I'll try to cheer him up.

I choose a glass he and his wife got as a wedding present, thinking it will be a nice reminder of the love they shared for one another, regardless of how things ended up, I suppose.

I carefully prepare the Old Fashioned, peeling an orange, zesting it, preparing the sugar cube and lighting it once I put the liquor inside the glass.

Pleased with my result, I place the pretty glass on a gold platter and carry it upstairs while still wearing the uniform Domenico picked for me.

I want him to be proud of me; look at me and realize I'm wearing the outfit *he chose.*

I wonder if he picked out this particular size just so he could watch me squirm. It's just a little too small for it to be an accident. After all, he had me measured for it.

I *think* I've caught him catching a glance a few times. But he *just* turned me down. I'm starting to second-guess myself.

There's no way he wants me.

I make my way to Domenico's office, platter shaky in my hands. I knock on the door and he calls for me to come in.

I'm not sure whether he's aware that we're finally the only two people left in the house now, but he doesn't say a word as I walk into the office and deposit the golden tray in front of him.

"My favorite drink, *ragazza*?" he asks, raising an eyebrow as if asking me a different kind of question altogether.

My body ignites at the forbidden fantasy.

"You thought you could drown my sorrows?" he answers for me. "That's a good idea. Thank you for taking care of me."

"Why did you send everyone away, Sir?" I ask shyly, and he looks away, his gaze troubled.

"I don't need people watching every step I take, judging me for how I grieve or don't grieve Arianna," he replies firmly. "The important thing is, she's gone. She won't be bossing anybody around anymore. Especially not you."

"Me?" My voice comes out squeaky.

"Yes," he says, taking a drink. "I'd rather get shot again than see her mistreat you, *ragazza*."

5

DOMENICO

"You've been shot, Sir?" she asks in a soft voice that sends my heart racing.

I approach her, standing up from the desk and taking her small hands in mine as I look into her eyes.

"You want to feel it?" I ask, guiding her hand over my chest to the trace of bullets that pierced my skin.

I let her feel the raised area of the scar tissue through the thin fabric of my shirt.

Vittoria gasps when she feels how deep the wounds go.

"Are you scared of me as much now?" I ask. "I'm not invincible. See?"

"I see, Sir."

"I'm sorry I neglected you last night. I have one last errand to run. We may have a visitor soon."

"A visitor?"

She backs away against the wall, but I'm not letting her get away that easily. Finally, we're alone, and nobody will stop me from taking what I want.

Least of all Vittoria, who seems more than excited to

become my sweet little toy—once she gets over the fear of someone walking in on us, that is.

She flattens her back against the wall and I approach her again, bracing my palms on either side of her head.

She's caged beneath my powerful body now with nowhere left to go.

I tip her chin back with one of my hands, forcing her to look up at me. I want her to tell me she's mine already, but I don't know if she quite realizes it yet.

I settle for growling a small warning in her ear.

"I've been waiting long enough, Vittoria. But just give me this one last task. Then you're all mine."

"Yours, Sir? Y-You like me too?"

"Of course I like you."

"Not that way, Sir, I..."

She pulls away, exposing her sweet biteable mouth to my lips as she looks up at me.

I desperately want to plunge in, to kiss her neck all the way up to her ears and taste her sweetness in all the right spots. But then I remember what I have to do first.

Vittoria's mother did one last shitty thing before I put her in the ground. Now I have to take care of it.

"I like you the way you want me to like you, I promise. I'm just a little bit distracted right now."

By the bastard who's about to ring my doorbell... and get a bullet in the head.

"First things first," I say gently. "You will call me Domenico from now on. Is that understood?"

"Yes, Sir-I mean, Domenico. Sir."

"Just Domenico," I remind her.

"Domenico," she whispers.

Our eyes meet and my heartbeat quickens. I raise my hand and gently stroke her cheek, trying to get a hold of my primal instincts.

Before I can stop myself, I'm holding her firmly in place as I lean in to take a better look at her. She's even more delicious up close.

I inhale the sweet essence of her scent as I pull her against me.

"Are you wearing perfume?" I ask.

"No," she whispers, and I smirk against her slender neck.

"One more thing," I whisper back. "That lipstick your mother gave you. Where is it?"

She pulls out a tacky tube with the offending makeup.

"You're sure you want me to like you?" I ask as I take the lipstick from her palm.

"I... Yes. I want you, Domenico."

My fingers trail down the front of her dress and she gasps as I slowly fold the edges of her collar away, exposing more of her inviting skin.

"You do?" I taunt her. "How important is this little trinket to you?"

I flash her the lipstick case and she looks up at me.

"It was my mother's..."

"And she was a bad person," I say through gritted teeth. "You will need to let go of her. Like this."

I toss the lipstick, case and all, into the fireplace.

Vittoria gasps.

"How could you do that, Sir?" She asks, crossing her arms.

"I told you to call me Domenico, and from this moment on, I expect you not to forget it again. Have we got a deal, Vittoria?"

She tries to turn away from me, but I'm too fast for her. My arms wrap around her waist and I pull her against me.

Before she can protest, I've already got my lips on hers, claiming her first kiss and making sure she remembers who she belongs to.

As my mouth devours hers, I feel her body arch against

mine in a desperate attempt to get closer to me. I get so hard it starts to hurt.

"You feel it too, don't you?" I whisper in her ear. "I can tell you do. This electricity between us..."

"No, Domenico!" She moans against my lips. "What would your wife say?"

"My wife is gone now," I remind her, a dark smile clouding my vision.

Fuck. Arianna is dead.

The finality of my words echoes in the room.

It didn't really hit me before, but now I'm overcome.

With elation, of course.

I can't believe I finally got rid of that shitty excuse for a human being.

"How long have you been hoping I would make you mine, *ragazza*?" I ask, raising my knowing eyes at her in anticipation of her answer.

For a moment I'm convinced she isn't going to reply, so I tug on one of her long red braids as a silent warning.

Vittoria flushes and I cherish the sight of redness in her cheeks.

Such innocence.

I want to put it in a bottle and hide it somewhere no one will ever find it.

"I've been desperate for all my first times to be with you," Vittoria finally admits, and I find myself groaning in the shell of her ear as she arches her body even more sharply to fit against mine.

I allow my hands to continue wandering down her back until they meet her ass.

The soft, supple globes are heavy in my hands as I groan and pull her up into my arms.

Instinctively, Vittoria's legs wrap around my waist and I

allow her to feel how excited she's making me as I push her up against the wall.

"I've wanted this for so long, Domenico," she whispers. "I finally don't have to fight it anymore... Is it true?"

"It's true."

I steal another kiss.

Her scent is driving me insane.

Vittoria smells like coconuts and peaches and I'm growing obsessed with it. It's fucking intoxicating and I'm desperate to have more of it in my mouth.

"I need to taste you," I tell her in a dark tone. "Have you had your pussy licked before?"

"No," she whispers. "I want you to be the first, Domenico..."

I pull her away from the wall and back towards the couch, where I place her down gently on the pillows and part her legs until she moans out loud.

I force myself to go slowly; to peel her panties to the side with painstaking precision until her gorgeous pussy is exposed to my hungry eyes.

At first, I only run my fingers over her slickness, and bring them to my mouth.

But not before inhaling their sweetness.

I suck on them to remind myself of the way she tastes now, before I take everything from her. Then I outline the shape of her clit with my fingertips, licking them every time I make a full circle.

By now, Vittoria is moaning, her back arching away from the couch as she desperately tries to get herself closer to me. I'm getting more and more turned on, but I keep reminding myself that I need to take it slow. If I've been patient for this long, I can handle it a little while longer.

But apparently, Vittoria cannot help herself.

"I don't want to call you Domenico," she whispers needily.

"What do you want to call me?" I tease her.

"Daddy."

The word rings out in the room, a shock to my whole fucking system, a goddamn dream come true.

"Please daddy," she whispers.

I'm so shocked that my heart threatens to beat out of my chest.

The sound of those words finally coming from her lips, completely unknown and unprovoked by me...

She is exactly who I thought she was.

A perfect woman.

Pulling her hips against me, I sink my lips against her wet entrance. I get my fill of licking her untouched pussy, lapping up her juices with my tongue until I'm filled with her taste.

I groan hungrily, pulling her deeper against me, desperately seeking out more of her sweetness.

"What did you just call me?" I ask. "Repeat it."

"No," she says, closing her eyes, her hands falling up to cover her blushing face. "I'm sorry."

I force her hands away from her eyes.

"Tell me who I am," I repeat, gently tickling her underneath her chin like before.

Vittoria looks up at me fearfully.

"Don't be afraid. I promise if I like it, I'll give you a reward. Do you want a reward?"

She eagerly nods. I'm mesmerized by her beauty, overtaken by the sheer perfection of this miraculous creature.

"Daddy," she whispers softly, and my cock stands at attention, poking at an angle that will make her fully aware of just how fucking hard I am.

Then, all of a sudden, the house doorbell rings.

"Fuck's sake."

I let go of her and rush to zip up my pants.

"Please wait for me right here, okay?"

I can't risk another distracting look at Vittoria.

I get out of the room and make my way down the stairs while reaching for the gun that's stuck into the waistband of my slacks.

I pull it out and click the trigger off.

I'm ready to shoot this bastard for what he tried to do to my Vittoria. No hesitation.

I open the front door and aim my gun at the sick bastard who's walked right into my trap.

His death will be the last on the list of people I killed to be with Vittoria, but I would kill a thousand more just to hear her call me daddy again.

I don't give a fuck about spilling blood when it comes to the woman I want forever.

"I've been expecting you," I say with a smile. "Why don't you come in? Tell me a little bit about yourself... and how you came to buy a girl's virginity online."

For the first time, I take a good look at him.

The customer.

He's balding with a fat beer belly to show for his clear drinking habit.

He doesn't say a word, just silently walks into the living room, clearly fidgety at the thought of what might happen.

"This isn't some kind of stupid show, right?" he asks. "The girl is here?"

I walk behind him, keeping the gun pointed in his direction.

"Much worse," I say politely.

When he sits down on the couch, I tell him matter-of-factly, "You're going to die here tonight, you fucker. In fact, I'm quite pleased that this is happening now, because I wanted to rush it along. You certainly got in the way enough already."

"Die? You don't have to kill me for it," he rushes to get out as his eyes finally take in the gun. "Wait! Wait... You're not Domenico Bianchi? Are you?"

"What difference does it make?"

"I've heard of you and your reputation. Everyone knows how ruthless you are, but—"

"You will be excellent proof to that," I interrupt. "What's a little more blood on my hands when it comes to my sweet Vittoria?"

"You are obsessed with this girl, Bianchi."

"Damn right I am," I hiss. "She's mine. That's why I had her conniving witch of a mother murdered. It's why I had my wife killed too. She got in the way. Just like you. Now it's your turn to die."

"You don't have to kill me! Please! I have a family!"

"You have a family?" I repeat, laughing as I sit down on the couch in front of him. "You have a family, and yet you still bet on an underage girl in an online auction put up by her mother?"

"She's eighteen now," he says, as if that absolves him.

"Don't give me that bullshit. You can't have her. She's mine."

I aim the gun at him when suddenly, something crashes in the hallway. I rip around, and the fucker takes it as his cue to make a run for it.

He dashes forward, and I turn back around just in time to take a shot at him... before I hear a different door slamming shut.

6

VITTORIA

I throw open the front door and take off toward the forest that surrounds the property. I can't believe what I've just heard and seen. The tall trees loom over the frozen ground as I rush through the winter chill, filled with dread.

Snow starts to fall as I run through the dense forest, my breaths coming in ragged gasps, my heart pounding against my ribcage. Twigs snap beneath my feet as I push myself to go faster, branches clawing at my skin in a desperate attempt to slow me down. But I can't stop, not when my life depends on it.

What Domenico said...

He killed two people to be with me, potentially three now...

Suddenly, the sound of an engine cuts through the night, headlights slicing through the darkness, momentarily blinding me. I skid to a halt, panic clawing at my throat as I stumble backward. The car screeches to a stop just a few feet in front of me, blocking any chance of escape.

Before I can react, a figure steps out from the driver's side, his silhouette ominous against the glaring lights. My heart races even faster as I try to make out any details, but all I see is the outline of a tall, powerful man.

"Please, I—" My plea is cut short as his strong arm reaches out, grabbing me roughly and pulling me towards the car. I struggle, fighting against his hold, but his grip is unyielding. With a swift, brutal movement, he strikes the back of my head, and my world spins into darkness.

When I finally regain consciousness, my head throbs with a dull ache. The rhythmic hum of the car's engine fills the silence, and the realization of my captivity hits me hard. I try to move, but my limbs feel heavy, my body sluggish from the blow.

The man sits stoically behind the wheel, his features obscured by shadows. Fear courses through me, mixing with the adrenaline that still lingers from the chase. I don't know what he wants, or why he's taken me, but the air crackles with a dangerous tension, thick with the unknown.

Every nerve in my body screams at me to fight, to find a way out, but the darkness closes in once more, pulling me into an abyss of unconsciousness. As I slip away, I cling to the hope that when I wake, I'll find a way to turn the tables, to escape the clutches of this enigmatic predator.

My eyelids flutter open, the world slowly coming back into focus. The rhythmic rocking of the car persists, a constant reminder of my captive state. My gaze darts around, panic rising within me as the memories flood back—the chase, the headlights, and the man who ambushed me.

I turn to face him, a surge of recognition hitting me like a punch to the gut. He's familiar—a guest at Domenico's house, one of those faces that blended into the background, someone I barely noticed. But now, under the harsh interior light of the car, every feature is etched in my mind.

"You..."

He grins, a lopsided smirk that does nothing to ease the unease gnawing at my insides. "Remember me, do you?"

My stomach churns as I take in his appearance—a balding head, a beer belly protruding from beneath his shirt. The contrast between him and the sinister aura he exudes only adds to the unsettling feeling crawling under my skin.

He's the man who was with my mother and Arianna in the apartment the day Mom died...

"What do you want from me?" I manage to choke out the question, my voice trembling despite my efforts to sound composed.

He chuckles darkly, the sound sending shivers down my spine. "Oh, don't play coy, Vittoria. You're the grand prize, didn't you know?"

His eyes gleam with a twisted excitement that makes my skin crawl.

My mind races, trying to make sense of his words. It all clicks into place—the underlying currents I had chosen to ignore. But I never imagined it would lead to this—a sick game where I'm the pawn.

A wave of revulsion washes over me, mingled with a newfound determination. I refuse to be reduced to an object, a commodity traded among these depraved individuals, headed by my mother.

"You think you can just—"

"Save your breath, darling." His dismissive tone cuts through my protest. "You're mine now, fair and square. I paid for you, and I intend to enjoy my prize."

Disgust claws at my throat, but I keep my expression neutral, masking the rising panic. I have to bide my time, find a way out of this nightmare. I'll play along until the perfect opportunity presents itself.

As the car rumbles on, his repulsive laughter echoes in the confined space, and I steel myself for the dangerous game ahead—a battle for my freedom against a man whose desires sicken me to the core.

I comply with his demand, closing my eyes tight, the darkness a thin veil against the horror I anticipate. But instead of the expected terror, the sharp crack of gunshots shatters the air, jolting me from my terror-induced trance.

My heart hammers against my chest, the sound reverberating through me, and then, an eerie silence descends. Uncertainty grips me, the seconds stretching into an eternity.

When I finally gather the courage to crack open my eyes, the scene before me sends my heart soaring. I'm not in the car anymore. Instead, I'm enveloped in Domenico's embrace, his arms a haven of safety and familiarity.

Alessio stands a few feet away, his laughter ringing out.

"Come on, man, that was the most pathetic attempt at a kidnapping I've ever seen!"

Relief washes over me, flooding my senses as I take in the surreal turn of events. Domenico's arms around me are like a shield, his presence grounding me in a reality where I'm not a prize to be won in some sick game.

I pull away slightly, meeting Domenico's eyes, the intensity of the moment not lost between us.

I don't know what this means for us. If there even is an *us*.

But he did just save my life. Surely that means his feelings are true?

Suddenly, through all the chaos, I realize what day it is.

"Christmas Eve," I breathe, the realization hitting me like a welcome avalanche.

Domenico smiles, a mixture of amusement and relief

dancing in his gaze. "Looks like our plans got a bit twisted, didn't they?"

Alessio joins in, his voice filled with teasing banter. "Well, at least we can say this year's Christmas has been eventful."

Despite the lingering unease from the ordeal, a warmth spreads through me. I'm back where I belong—wrapped in Domenico's arms, surrounded by the banter of his closest friend...

Who killed my mother.

As we make our way back to Domenico's, the car filled with laughter and playful banter, I can't shake off the residual tremors of fear.

I don't trust Alessio.

But the overwhelming joy of being reunited with Domenico on this special night eclipses everything else. This Christmas Eve, despite the chaos, feels like a miracle—a moment of profound gratitude for the love and safety I've found in his arms.

Domenico's invitation for Alessio to stay for Christmas dinner is met with a polite refusal. Alessio insists he has pressing matters to attend to, a knowing glint in his eye hinting at a hidden agenda. With a playful wink, he bids us farewell, leaving Domenico and me alone in the quiet embrace of the night.

As the door shuts behind Alessio, Domenico turns to me, his eyes holding a tenderness that sends a rush of warmth through me. He scoops me up effortlessly, cradling me in his arms as we make our way into the house.

The warmth inside envelops us, the scent of pine and spices mingling in the air, a cozy contrast to the chilly night outside. Domenico carries me with a gentle strength that speaks of protection and adoration, his gaze never leaving mine.

I trace the outline of his features, the familiarity of his touch grounding me after the harrowing events of the evening.

As we pass beneath the mistletoe hanging in the hallway, I meet his gaze, a silent understanding passing between us.

Without a word, he leans in, his lips meeting mine in a tender, lingering kiss. It's a promise of safety, of unwavering devotion amidst the chaos that often encircles us. The world outside fades away, leaving only the warmth of his embrace, the softness of his lips against mine.

When we finally part, a soft smile plays on Domenico's lips, a silent reassurance in the midst of unspoken emotions. He carries me further into the house, into the heart of our sanctuary, where the flickering lights of the Christmas tree cast a gentle glow over everything.

"We need to talk," I whisper as he presents me with a hot chocolate. "About what I found out..."

"It's true," Domenico says. "I had your mother killed. As well as Arianna."

"But *why?*"

"Because they were horrible people with even worse intentions," he grits out. "Your own mother was ready to sell your virginity. What else would she have done if I didn't intervene?"

"And Arianna?" I bite my lips nervously. "You were married..."

"Only on paper. It wasn't anything real... unlike this. Like you."

My heart skips a beat and I do my best to hide my shaky smile.

Finally, I have someone to kiss under the mistletoe.

Domenico asks me to get my things from the guest suite.

"Am I moving rooms again?"

"Yes," he says nonchalantly. "Since you're mine now, you will share a room with me."

Shocked by how easily he made the decision, I nod and quickly gather my things. He helps me move my meager belongings to the primary suite and I nervously sit on the edge of the bed, the events of the previous few days still on my mind.

"Are you comfortable with me, Vittoria?"

His question catches me off-guard. Even though I know I shouldn't, I find myself nodding.

"Good girl." He gently tips my chin back and makes me look up at him. "So pretty."

I let out a moan when he touches the swelling in his pants.

"We got interrupted last time," he growls. "But we won't tonight. Take your clothes off."

I follow suit, quickly getting rid of everything on me. I'm more than eager to strip off the dirty clothes. But I'm even more eager for Domenico to touch me again.

His fingers outline my hip bones, sliding down past my belly button. I gasp when he reaches my pussy. Domenico's eyes are still locked on mine, and it's driving me insane.

"Please," I whimper, already needy for his touch.

"What do you want?" He's teasing me again, and I've fallen right into his trap. The silver in his blue eyes shines with a mischievous darkness. It's a ruthless twinkle that I could get lost in for days.

"Inside..."

"Inside where?"

I can't take it. My whole body is shaking, I'm so desperate. I take his fingers and push down. As soon as he feels my pussy lips beneath his fingertips, he tries to back up, but I won't let him. I guide his hand, tracing them as he breathes fire down my neck.

"You're fucking soaked," he says. His eyes are still on mine, and I'm blushing.

"Please just..." I'm struggling to get the words out, and my cheeks are burning up. I feel embarrassed as hell, but I have to tell him. I can't keep it to myself. "Be gentle."

"Why?" he asks roughly. His calloused fingers are parting

my lips now, and I'm wriggling on his lap. I feel something building up inside me. It's dangerous. It makes me want to break for him, shatter to pieces just so he can put me back together. I need this so badly.

"I... I've never done this before." I'm going to faint. I can't stand this. "I'm a virgin."

"I know," he smirks. "I made sure of it. That changes tonight. With me."

Domenico stops, but his fingers are still holding me open.

"Don't stop," I beg him. "Don't stop, please, please, please..."

"Fuck," he breathes. I feel his teeth grazing my skin, and I almost lose it. I can tell he's holding back, and I want to scream at him to stop doing it. I need him to lose control. Right. Fucking. *Now.*

I buck my hips against his, my shaky hands reaching down between my legs. I grab his arm, guiding it to my center. He looks down this time, his finger wandering between my folds.

"Fuck me," I beg him.

His other hand digs into my back. "Not yet. Not until you call me what you called me last time. Do you remember, Vittoria?"

I blush at his words, but my body obeys, nodding.

"I don't want to hurt you."

"Please." My voice is embarrassingly husky. "Please."

"Please what?"

I hesitate. I want to be done with the begging, but at the same time, it's doing things to me. Things I'd be embarrassed to admit out loud—though I'm fairly certain he'll make me do it anyway.

"F-Fuck me," I manage to get out.

"It will hurt."

"That's okay."

"I'm not gentle."

"I know."

"I won't change that for you."

"I don't want you to."

He lets go of me and I nearly tumble to the floor. I turn around, shaking all over. Domenico pulls his shirt off, and I gasp when I see his skin. He's ripped, and his body is covered with scars. Some running deep, some barely healed.

"Come here," he orders me. I do as he says. "Undress me."

It's a test. He's trying to show me I'm not ready for this. I give him a determined look, trying to pretend I don't feel vulnerable in front of him when he's clothed and I'm naked.

My hands shake as I reach for his belt. The metal is loud as I unbuckle it and slide down his jeans. He's wearing skin tight navy boxers, which don't hide his erection at all. He's massive.

"All the way, Vittoria," Domenico growls.

His hands have formed fists at his sides and I can tell he's barely holding back. Hesitantly, I slide down his boxers and his cock springs free. He's huge, veiny and throbbing for me. I gasp as Domenico wraps his fingers in my hair, pushing me to my knees.

"Suck me first," he says. "Make it sloppy. I want that pretty face dirtied up."

I'm scared at the prospect of putting his dick inside my mouth. I doubt I can even wrap my fingers around it. Tentatively, I reach for him and take him in my hand at the base of his cock. He groans, and I feel the strangest kind of pressure building in my center. It's intense, almost to the point of making me dizzy. I crawl closer on my knees and look up at Domenico. He's throbbing in my hand, and his hand is holding my head in place firmly.

"I don't know h-how," I stutter, licking my lips. I would be scared if it weren't for that pressure, the tension building inside me. But it feels so damn good. I feel hot and woozy, almost like I'm getting drunk on it.

"Lick," Domenico tells me. "Start at the base. Make your way up. Work that little pussy while you do it."

I blush at his crude words, but I know I'll do exactly what he tells me. I lean in, and my lips touch his base. It's silky, but firm. I moan against his cock and his fingers tighten in my hair. I start licking in careful, tentative strokes. Slow licks to get familiar with his taste. I moan against his shaft, because I am weak, and I can't hold back.

My shaky fingers find their way between my legs and I press down on my core. I'm moaning before I've even found my clit.

"That's a good girl," Domenico coos. "Spread your legs. Let me see."

I obey blindly, my knees going apart, so he can see me touching myself. Both his hands are wrapped in my hair now, and my fingers are seeking out that little button that's throbbing in my center, so fucking desperate to be touched, pinched and flicked.

I part my lips and he pulls down on my hair. My fingers find that spot, that fucking spot that makes me lose all inhibition, just as he plunges his cock inside my mouth. I try to squirm free, but his grip on me is tight. His cock is huge, filling up my whole mouth and making my eyes tear up as he hits the back of my throat. But I'm still touching myself, with my free hand braced on Domenico's thighs. I could push him away easily enough, but I choose not to.

"Good girl," he praises me. "Let me fuck that pretty little face."

My eyes widen as he pushes inside, then out, and back in. My throat is slowly adjusting to his length and girth, and finally, I find myself enjoying it. Just like that, I'm back in the zone, my fingers strumming my clit, so fucking ready to come. He fucks my face slowly, groaning with each thrust of his hips. A few tears roll down my cheeks, but I'm past the point of caring. I'm so close, so fucking close. I feel like I'm going to burst any minute now.

"Fuck," Domenico curses out loud. "You feel so good. Your mouth wrapped around my cock like that. Fuck, you are beautiful."

Finally, his fingers touch my wetness, the wet folds of my pussy. I moan. "I-I won't be able to go much longer," I breathe heavily.

He grabs me by the waist and presses his body dangerously close to mine, and I shake all over. "You come when I tell you to," he growls at me. "Not a moment sooner. Do you understand?"

My eyes are wide and glazed over as I look up at him. I nod silently, begging with my expression for him to go on. And mercifully, he does.

He holds me in place by grabbing onto my waist and gets between my legs. They wrap around his waist instinctively, and I whisper for him to go on. Taking his thickness in one hand, he positions his cock at my entrance. I'm scared, but I still beg him to push inside.

Domenico looks up at me one last time, his eyes asking me if I'm sure. Instead of answering, I break the rules, my arms go down and I guide him inside me. He exhales in shock and pleasure as his tip pushes inside me. Intense pain takes hold of my body, sharp and stinging. My breath catches in my throat and a tear spills from my eyes, but then Domenico's hands are on my face, and he's looking at me, and I feel his love, his devotion, and everything he feels for me.

We wait like that until my body adjusts to the intrusion; until my whimpers turn into moans. And then he starts moving, thrusting ever so slowly, stretching me.

"Oh my god," I whimper. My back arches again. I need him closer. Deeper. Harder. "Fuck. More. Please more."

I can tell he's holding back, and he grits his teeth as he

starts pushing inside me. Every thrust of his hips is an effort, because I can tell he wants to go so much harder. But he holds back as much as he can, until my begging becomes too much. And then he really starts fucking me.

Deep thrusts, hitting a spot inside me I didn't even know was there. He doesn't take his eyes from mine as he fucks me, and I stare back at him, mesmerized. I pushed him away for so long. For *too* long I was without this closeness, without feeling him inside me.

"Does it hurt?" he asks me softly.

I close my eyes for a second and nod slowly. "It's good..."

He groans, as if those words were too much for him. And he goes harder. I can feel him growing thicker, throbbing in my pussy, and I know I did that. It's enough to push me over the edge. I feel myself moaning louder, my breaths coming in faster, needing his release.

"Vittoria," he breathes into my hair. "Don't come without me, my little girl..."

My breath hitches in my throat and I hold it, as if I'm holding the door closed on the feelings that are banging on the other side, so desperate to get out. A long, sensual moan escapes my lips and I open my cloudy eyes.

"Daddy," I whisper.

Domenico grins before kissing me, a soft touch of his lips against mine, his tongue touching the tip of mine. "Come for me now."

The last straw is feeling his cock throb inside me, and that pushes me over the edge. His fingers coil around my hair and he pumps fast. A groan escapes him, and I know he's going to cum just like me.

And finally, I focus on the storm inside me. It feels as if something's ripping me apart and putting me together at the same time. I let go, and for the first time, it doesn't scare me to fall to pieces.

We come together. His hands in my hair, mine scratching his back. In this moment, our fates are sealed. I am his, and he is mine, and that will never change. I belong to him completely now.

One final thrust, one final look, and he finishes with a groan. I'm kissing him even though I feel like I'm about to pass out. Long licks with our tongues, moaning against each other's lips. He bites down on my bottom lip and I moan as I feel his cock throb inside me.

"Such a pretty girl for daddy."

EPILOGUE
DOMENICO

The next day, on Christmas, I watch Alessio work with meticulous precision, his hands steady as he etches Vittoria's likeness onto the canvas of my skin. She sits across from us, her eyes fixed on the process, a mix of amusement and curiosity dancing in her gaze.

"So, Alessio," I begin, leaning back against the chair, a smirk tugging at the corners of my lips, "is this your way of making sure Vittoria's always on my mind?"

Alessio chuckles, his focus unwavering as the tattoo gun moves gracefully across my skin. "Well, Domenico, I figured you needed a constant reminder of the trouble you got yourself into."

His tone drips with playful sarcasm.

Vittoria's laughter echoes through the room, a sound that brings warmth to my chest.

"Oh, I'm trouble, am I?"

Her voice teases, but there's a glint of mischief in her eyes.

I meet her gaze, a silent exchange passing between us, filled with unspoken affection and a depth of understanding that transcends words.

"You two are quite the pair," Alessio remarks, his grin widening as he adds the finishing touches to the tattoo. "There, all done."

I glance at the mirror to my side, catching a glimpse of the intricate portraits of Vittoria that now cover my body. Alessio's talent never fails to astound me—the details capture her essence, her spirit, in a way that words can't express.

Vittoria leans in, examining the tattoos with a playful smirk.

"Not bad, Alessio. I might have to start charging you royalties for the use of my likeness."

Alessio feigns offense, placing a hand dramatically over his heart.

"But of course, my dear Vittoria. Your image is priceless."

The banter fills the room, a comfortable camaraderie settling between us. Despite the darkness that often encircles our lives, these moments of lightheartedness and playful teasing bring a sense of normalcy—a reminder that amidst chaos, there's room for laughter and love.

As the evening unfolds, we find ourselves wrapped in an easy companionship, the closeness of our bond evident in the shared jokes and knowing glances. It's moments like these that make me cherish what we have—the unbreakable bond between friends and the deep, undeniable connection I share with Vittoria.

Darkness may linger at the edges of our world, but here, in this moment, in the glow of the tattoo studio, there's only the warmth of laughter and the promise of unwavering companionship.

I shoot Alessio a mischievous grin. "Speaking of faces on skin, how's Liliana? Still trying to get her portrait inked?"

Alessio's smirk falters slightly, a flicker of irritation crossing his features before he shrugs it off. "I'm taking my time with it, you know, making sure it's perfect."

"What's holding you back?"

His back stiffens, his mouth tightening as he glances at Vittoria.

"My brother."

Matteo's name hangs in the air unspoken, a bittersweet echo of memories and heartfelt emotions. Alessio, Matteo, and I—bound by friendship, tangled in a web of shared history. I glance at Alessio, catching the fleeting sadness that clouds his eyes before he shields it with a practiced facade.

Vittoria's curiosity breaks the tension, her voice soft as she asks, "Who's your brother?"

Alessio's response is cryptic, a mix of melancholy and finality.

"He's no one, Vittoria. Just a ghost from the past."

He finishes his work, packing up his equipment with practiced efficiency. Alessio's departure feels like the closing of a chapter, leaving behind unanswered questions and lingering emotions.

As the door closes behind him, I'm left admiring the intricate tapestry of ink that adorns my skin—the stories, the memories, the pain, and the laughter woven into every design. Vittoria's arms wrap around me in a comforting embrace, a silent reassurance amidst the echoes of the evening.

"Do you like it?" I ask Vittoria, showing off the tattoos that now bear her face.

"It's lovely," she says softly. "So, are you serious about this, then?"

"What do you think, Vittoria?" he smirks.

"I'm not sure…"

"Let me prove it to you then."

I let go of her hands and kneel before her. Vittoria's hands fly up to cover her mouth.

"I've done a lot of bad shit in my life," I say solemnly. "But all with a goal in mind. This time, my goal was to make you mine. *My little girl.*"

She flushes as I pull out a box from the inner pocket of my jacket.

"I know it's soon and unexpected, but I want you to be mine. Forever," I murmur. "Vittoria, will you marry me and make me the happiest man in this dark and twisted world?"

"No," she grins, and my heart falters. "I'll make you the happiest *daddy*."

I grin as I slip the ring on her finger and she admires how the rubies and diamonds glint in the light.

"It's so beautiful, Domenico. The red stones remind me of something. They look like..."

"Mistletoe?"

"Exactly!"

"What can I say," I smirk. "I'm a sucker for a Christmas romance."

THE END

Want to read more about Alessio? Well, good news! He has his own full-length novel.

DEVIL'S LILY

Printed in Great Britain
by Amazon